Enjoy all of the Princess Posey books

PRINCESS P🌸SEY
and the
FIRST GRADE PLAY

Stephanie Greene

ILLUSTRATED BY
Stephanie Roth Sisson

G. P. PUTNAM'S SONS

G. P. PUTNAM'S SONS
an imprint of Penguin Random House LLC
375 Hudson Street
New York, NY 10014

Text copyright © 2017 by Stephanie Greene.
Illustrations copyright © 2017 by Stephanie Roth Sisson.
Penguin supports copyright. Copyright fuels creativity, encourages
diverse voices, promotes free speech, and creates a vibrant culture.
Thank you for buying an authorized edition of this book and for complying
with copyright laws by not reproducing, scanning, or distributing any part of it
in any form without permission. You are supporting writers and allowing
Penguin to continue to publish books for every reader.

G. P. Putnam's Sons is a registered trademark of Penguin Random House LLC.

Library of Congress Cataloging-in-Publication Data is available upon request.

Printed in the United States of America.
ISBN 9780399175688
1 3 5 7 9 10 8 6 4 2

Decorative graphics by Marikka Tamura. Design by Marikka Tamura.
Text set in Stempel Garamond.
This is a work of fiction. Names, characters, places, and incidents either are
the product of the author's imagination or are used fictitiously, and
any resemblance to actual persons, living or dead, businesses, companies,
events, or locales is entirely coincidental.

For teachers, everywhere.

—S.G.

To Tristam Sisson, who

loves the stage.

—S.R.S.

CONTENTS

BEE EXPERTS

"What else have we learned about bees?" Miss Lee asked.

Hands around the classroom shot up.

"Grace?" said Miss Lee.

"Bees die after they sting you," Grace said.

"And why do bees sting?" Miss Lee asked. "Henry?"

"Because birds and frogs try to eat them," Henry said. "It's called self-defense."

"Right. What else?" Miss Lee looked around. "Posey?"

"Bees carry pollen from flower to flower," Posey said.

"How? With their hands?" Miss Lee asked.

Posey laughed. "Bees don't have hands," she said.

"It sticks to their fuzzy bodies," said Nikki.

"I'm impressed. You have all become bee experts," Miss Lee said.

Two girls at one table were giggling with each other.

"Caitlyn and Rashmi?" said Miss Lee. The girls looked up. "Is there something you would like to share with the class?"

"Caitlyn has a funny eraser," Rashmi said.

"Why don't you show the whole class, Caitlyn," said Miss Lee.

Caitlyn held up a small yellow eraser. It was in the shape of a bee. It had black stripes and wings.

"That's sooooo cute," Grace whispered to Posey.

"My mother gave it to me because I know so much about bees," Caitlyn said.

"It's very nice, but it belongs in your cubby," said Miss Lee. "Go and put it there now, please."

While Caitlyn went to her cubby, Miss Lee said, "The rest of

you can go and get your books. It's silent reading time."

Everyone rushed to get their books and claim their favorite place to read. A group of girls stood in front of Caitlyn's cubby.

"Let me see! Lee me see!" they all said.

Posey, Ava, Nikki, and Grace joined them.

"That's so cute," Ava said. "Can I hold it?"

Caitlyn held the eraser against her chest. "Only my best friends can hold it."

"Who cares about an old eraser?" Posey said as they walked away.

"I really like it," Ava said.

"Me, too," said Grace.

"Caitlyn gets everything she wants," Nikki said.

Last week, Caitlyn wore green cowgirl boots to school. She said she was taking horse-riding lessons.

"Caitlyn's spoiled," Posey said.

"I still wish I had a bee eraser," said Ava.

Posey wished she had one, too.

THE WIGGLE-WAGGLE DANCE

Posey went to Nikki's house to play after school. When she got home, her mom was making dinner.

"Hi. Did you have a good time?" her mom asked.

"Nikki's dad helped us make pizza," said Posey. "It was so much fun."

"You are just in time to set the table," said her mom.

Posey took the forks out of the drawer.

"You know what, Mom?" she asked.

"What?"

"Bees can dance."

"They can?"

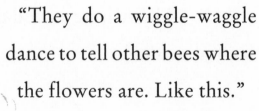 "They do a wiggle-waggle dance to tell other bees where the flowers are. Like this."

Posey wiggled her
bottom from side to
side.

Her mom laughed.

"You know what else?" said Posey. "There's only one queen bee in the hive, but there are *thousands* of worker bees. A thousand is a lot."

"It sure is," her mom said.

Posey told her about Caitlyn's eraser. "Can I get one?" she asked.

"This is Danny's birthday week," her mom said. "If we buy anything, it should be for him, don't you think?"

Posey frowned.

Her mom took the chicken out

of the oven. "Go wiggle-waggle and tell him it's time for dinner."

Danny was playing with his dump truck on the living room floor. His colored blocks were scattered everywhere.

Posey picked up a block and put it in the truck.

Danny roared.

"It's time to clean up," Posey told him. She picked up another block.

"Mine!" Danny shouted.

"Danny, it's time for dinner," Posey said.

Her mom came to the living room door. "What's the matter?" she asked.

"Danny's being spoiled," said Posey.

"Oh, don't be mean. He's the birthday boy." Her mom swooped Danny up and kissed him. "On Sunday, he will be two, two, two. Won't you, Danny?"

She poked him in the stomach three times.

Danny laughed and grabbed her finger.

"I didn't get a whole week for my birthday," said Posey.

"Sure you did. You got to choose a different flavor ice cream cone

every day of the week, remember?"
said her mom.

"That was a long time ago,"
Posey grumbled.

Her mom laughed. "Be a good
girl and clean up the blocks while I
wash Danny's hands," she said.

CHAPTER THREE

PUTTING ON A PLAY

"**H**urry and sit down," Miss Lee told the class the next morning. "I have something to tell you. I think you are going to like it."

Posey stuffed her backpack into her cubby and went to the carpet. Grace was already there.

Miss Lee waited until everyone was seated.

"Last night, I was thinking about how much you all like bees," she said. "So we're going to put on a play to show the other first grade classes what you have learned."

A play! Their class had never put on a play!

Posey and Grace squeezed hands.

"A real live play!" Posey said.

"I want to be a bee that makes honey," said Rashmi. "I love honey!"

"I want to be a guard bee," said Luca. He made muscles in his arms like he was strong. "*Bzzz . . .*"

Everyone else buzzed, too.

The room sounded like a beehive.

Miss Lee laughed. "All right, boys and girls. Calm down."

When they were quiet again, Miss Lee told them about the play.

Some of them would be the worker bees that clean the hive or take care of the babies, she said. Others would be the guard bees that protect the hive.

Some of them would be the bees that collect pollen to make honey.

"I will let you know on Monday which bees you're going to be," Miss Lee said. "Everyone will get a part to play."

Posey was so excited.

She was worried, too.

Only one person could be the queen bee.

Posey wanted that more than anything.

CHAPTER
FOUR

POSEY'S HEART
IS SET

osey told Gramps about the play on the way home.

"I hope I'm the queen bee," she said.

"I thought a queen bee was someone who is bossy," said Gramps.

"She's the best one. All of the other bees take care of her."

"What about the king bee? Who takes care of him?"

"They don't have a king bee," said Posey.

"No fair!" said Gramps.

When Posey got home, the kitchen was empty.

"Mom! Where are you?" she shouted.

"I'm up here!" her mom called.

Posey ran upstairs. Her mom was giving Danny a bath. He had green bubbles in his hair and on his face. Her mom had green bubbles in her hair, too. There were green streaks on her shirt.

"What happened?" Posey asked.

"Danny got into the finger paints," said her mom. "Luckily, I caught him before he could paint the wall."

"Guess what?" Posey said. "We're putting on a play about bees!"

"That sounds like fun."

"I want to be the queen bee," Posey said.

"I'm sure a lot of other girls want to be, too," said her mom. "Don't get your heart set on it."

It was too late. Posey's heart was already set.

She had the perfect thing to wear, too.

She went into her bedroom and

put on her tutu and her veil with
sparkles.

She stood
in front of
the mirror.

"I am the queen. You have to obey me!" she commanded in her best queen voice.

It would be so much fun.

JUST DANNY
AND GRAMPS

On Saturday morning, Posey was watching cartoons when Gramps arrived. She went into the kitchen.

Gramps was helping Danny put on his coat.

"Where are you going?" Posey asked.

"I'm taking Danny to see some trucks," said Gramps. "They're building a new wing on the hospital. There are backhoes and bulldozers everywhere."

"Can I come?"

"This is a boys' day out, sport," said Gramps. "An early birthday present."

"Just you and Danny?" said Posey. "But it's you and me who do special things on Saturday."

"Darn right. Our Special Saturdays. That's not going to change," Gramps said.

"Posey, you don't even like trucks," said her mom.

"I do, too," Posey said in a small voice.

Gramps hugged her. "We'll be back in no time," he said.

Posey got on the living room couch when they left. She looked out the window as Gramps buckled Danny into his car seat.

Then Gramps got into his truck

and backed slowly out of the driveway. The truck disappeared down the street.

Posey's eyes stung. She blinked fast.

Danny had Gramps all to himself.

Posey wished she didn't even have a baby brother.

She sank down on the couch and crossed her arms.

Her mom came to the door.

"Why don't you invite a friend over?" she asked.

"I don't feel like it," said Posey.

"Then come and help me make Danny's cake."

"Why should I, when you won't buy me a bee eraser?"

Her mom looked at Posey for a minute. "You're being silly," she said. "I'll be in the kitchen if you need me."

Posey frowned at the empty room.

She didn't like her mom and Gramps anymore. All they cared about was Danny.

No one cared about her.

THE ERASER

On Monday morning, Miss Lee stood at the front of the room. She was holding a bag.

"I put everyone's name on a slip of paper," Miss Lee told them.

She shook the bag. "I'm going to take them out to see which bee you're going to play."

How exciting! It was like a game.

"What if a boy gets the queen bee?" Ava asked.

"Then we'll let him decide what he wants to do," said Miss Lee. "Ready?"

"Ready!" they all cried.

"Listen carefully so you hear your name when I read it. The first group will be the bees who

take care of the babies." Miss Lee
took out the first slip of paper.

She called Ava's name. Ava clapped her hands.

Miss Lee continued to take out names for each group.

Luca and Nikki were worker bees.

Henry was in the group of bees that make honey.

Then Miss Lee picked names for the bees that tell the other bees where the flowers are. "Rashmi . . . and Grace . . . ," she said.

Posey squeezed her eyes shut. *Not me, not me, not me . . .*

" . . . and Posey."

Posey's shoulders slumped.

Miss Lee took out the last slip of paper. "Caitlyn, you will be the queen bee."

No fair!

Caitlyn got everything.

Everyone around Posey was talking excitedly.

Grace bounced up and down in her chair. "You and me are together!" she said. "It will be so fun!"

Posey didn't think it sounded fun.

"Now I want to show you the hat you're all going to make for your costumes," said Miss Lee.

She held up the hat.

The headband was made out of yellow paper. Black and yellow pipe cleaners were twisted together to make two antennae.

The antennae stood straight up in the air. Each one had a yellow pom-pom at the tip.

"If you have anything to put away, go to your cubby now,"

Miss Lee said. "Then come and get your paper and pipe cleaners."

Posey hurried to her cubby. Caitlyn's cubby was in the row under hers.

The bee eraser was on top of Caitlyn's lunch box.

Posey's mouth turned down when she saw it.

Why should Caitlyn have the eraser when she got to be queen bee, too?

Posey picked the eraser up and put it in her pack.

THE TERRIBLE MISTAKE

"Don't you want your cookies?" Nikki said at lunch.

"I don't feel good," said Posey.

"Do you want me to tell Miss Lee?" Ava asked.

Posey shook her head.

When they went back to their classroom, Miss Lee was in the corner, talking to Caitlyn.

Caitlyn's shoulders were shaking.

"Something's wrong with Caitlyn," Grace whispered.

"I think she's crying," said Ava.

Posey and Grace quietly sat at their table.

Miss Lee put her arm around Caitlyn's shoulders and turned to the class.

"Boys and girls," she said, "I need your help."

Everyone stopped talking.

Caitlyn gave a loud sniff.

"Caitlyn's bee eraser is missing," said Miss Lee. "She put it in her cubby, but now it's not there."

The bad feeling in Posey's stomach got stronger.

"Caitlyn is upset. It was her special eraser," Miss Lee said. "She's sad that she can't find it."

Everyone looked serious.

"I want you to look on the floor around your tables," Miss

Lee said. "Check your cubbies, too, in case Caitlyn put it in the wrong one."

Posey and Grace looked on the floor. They checked their cubbies.

Posey didn't know what to do. She wished she could put the eraser back. But what if someone saw her?

"That's enough for now," Miss Lee called. "We'll hope Caitlyn's eraser turns up tomorrow."

They all went back to their tables.

"What if someone *stole* it?" said Grace.

Posey's eyes got wide. That was such a scary word.

Only bad people stole things.

When she took the eraser, it had felt good.

Now it felt like a terrible mistake, deep inside.

CHAPTER
EIGHT

"I DIDN'T MEAN TO"

Gramps was waiting for Posey in the car pick-up line.

"Your mom thinks you felt a little left out on Saturday," he said on the way home. "You're my number one girl, you know that."

Posey didn't say anything.

"How about if you and I work

on a project together? Just the two of us."

"Like what?"

"You'll see."

Gramps pulled into Posey's driveway. They went into the house. A huge cardboard box stood in the middle of the living room.

"Ta-da!" said Gramps.

"What is it?" Posey asked.

"It was for a refrigerator, but we are going to make that book house you talk about so much. The special place where you can read your books."

All Posey did was look at it.

"What's wrong? You don't seem

very excited," said Gramps.

"I have a stomachache," Posey said.

"Why don't you lie down for a bit?" Gramps said. "Your mom will be home soon."

Posey went up to her room. She took the bee eraser out of her pack and crouched beside her bed. She pushed the eraser under the mattress as far back as she could.

Then she got under the covers.

Maybe if she couldn't see it, she wouldn't think about it.

Posey closed her eyes.

It didn't work.

❀ ❀ ❀

"Posey?" Her mom came into the room and sat on the edge of Posey's bed. "Gramps said you don't feel well."

She put her hand on Posey's forehead. "You don't have a temperature," she said.

Posey's eyes filled with tears. "I didn't mean to," she sobbed.

"Mean to what?" her mom asked.

It all came out in a jumble.

"All right, calm down," her mom said when Posey was finished. "Where is the eraser now?"

Posey got out of bed and pulled it from under the mattress. She put it in her mom's hand.

"All of those tears for such a tiny thing." Her mom sounded sad.

"I don't even like it anymore," Posey said.

"It's wrong to take something that doesn't belong to you. You know that," said her mom.

"But Caitlyn—"

"No. No *buts*."

Posey wiped her eyes with the backs of her hands.

"In this family, we do not take things from other people. No matter how much we want them," her mom said.

Posey sniffed.

"What you did is not as important as what you do now to fix it."

"What?"

"You need to return it to Caitlyn and tell her you're sorry."

"But everyone will think I'm bad!" Posey cried.

"Talk to Miss Lee first. She will help you work it out," her mom said.

"Can you talk to her?" Posey asked.

"No." Her mom kissed her forehead. "I love you very much, Posey, but this is something you did. You need to fix it."

Her mom went downstairs.

Posey took her tutu out of her drawer and hugged it to her like a blanket.

She was so scared.

She wished she could wear her tutu to school tomorrow. Posey never told anyone, but when she wore her tutu, she was Princess Posey.

Princess Posey was brave. She could go anywhere and do anything.

Posey wasn't sure she could be brave all by herself.

AN APOLOGY

The next morning, Posey walked quietly up to Miss Lee's desk.

"Miss Lee?" she said.

"Good morning." Miss Lee's smile disappeared when she saw Posey's face. "What's wrong?"

Posey took her hand out of her pocket. She put the bee eraser on Miss Lee's desk.

"Caitlyn's eraser!" Miss Lee sounded surprised. "Where did you find it?"

"It was a mistake," Posey said in a small voice.

"Oh. I see," said Miss Lee.

"I didn't mean to take it, but I wanted it," Posey said. Her lower lip trembled. "I have to tell Caitlyn I'm sorry."

"I can see you're sorry, Posey," Miss Lee said. "It was hard for you to come and tell me about it, wasn't it?"

Posey nodded.

"It was very brave, and I think one apology is enough." Miss Lee opened her drawer and dropped in the eraser. "I will give it to Caitlyn when she gets here. I know she'll be happy to see it."

That was it.

Posey couldn't believe it.

Miss Lee stood up.

"I'm going to ask one child from each group in the play to say something about what their bees do," she said. "Do you think you can do that for the wiggle-waggle group?"

Posey nodded again.

"Then go and put your things away," Miss Lee said. "We have a lot to do if we're going to put on a play this Friday."

Posey went to her cubby. She wanted to do her own wiggle-waggle dance for everyone to see. It would tell them, *Miss Lee is the best teacher in the world!*

KIDS ONLY

"How was the play?" Posey's mom asked when Posey came home from school on Friday.

"Great!" Posey dumped her things on the kitchen table. "Miss Lee played music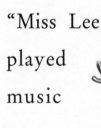

called 'Flight of the Bumblebee.' It sounded like real bees flying."

"That must have been fun."

"It was so fast! We danced all around, like this." Posey ran in circles and wiggled her bottom back and forth. Her mom laughed.

"It was so fast, I got dizzy,"
Posey said when she stopped. "The
queen didn't get to do anything.
All she did was sit."

"Did you remember your line?"
her mom asked.

"'Honeybees do a wiggle-waggle dance to tell other bees where the flowers are,'" Posey recited.

"Good job," said her mom.

Danny came into the kitchen and held up a book to Posey. "Book wead," he said.

"He's been waiting for you all afternoon," said her mom.

"Okay. Come on," Posey said.

The box was in one corner of the living room. Gramps had helped Posey cut out windows and a door. She covered the outside with rainbows and flowers. She painted the door blue.

A sign above the door read

POSEY'S BOOK HOUSE

KIDS ONLY

"Maybe I'll put your name on the sign, too, Danny. Would you like that?" Posey opened the door and crawled over to the pile of pillows in one corner.

Danny crawled in behind her. He settled next to her and put his book in her lap. Then he stuck his thumb in his mouth.

"I'm Gramps's number one girl, and you're his number one boy," Posey told him. "But never take something from someone. Our family doesn't do that, okay?"

Danny said, "Wead," with his thumb still in his mouth.

"I knew it," Posey sighed. "Another truck book."

She opened the book and started to read. It felt as cozy as the inside of a beehive.

Watch for the next **PRINCESS POSEY** book!

PRINCESS
P●SEY
and the
FLOWER GIRL
FIASCO

Posey thinks Gramps marrying Mrs. Romero is the most exciting thing ever, and she is going to be their flower girl. But when she learns about some of the changes that will come after the wedding, suddenly it doesn't seem like a good idea anymore. Can Princess Posey's tutu help her get used to all of the changes?